For Annette with my love
A.M.

For my parents with thanks
for the love and support
M.B.

Text copyright © 1990 Angela McAllister
Illustrations copyright © 1990 Michaela Bloomfield

All rights reserved.

CIP data is available.

First published in the United States 1990 by
Dutton Children's Books,
a division of Penguin Books USA Inc.

Published simultaneously in Canada by
Fitzhenry & Whiteside Limited, Toronto

Originally published in 1990 by
Aurum Books for Children
33 Museum Street, London WC1A 1LD

First American Edition   Printed and bound in Italy by LEGO
ISBN: 0-525-44616-8   10 9 8 7 6 5 4 3 2 1

WHEN THE ARK WAS FULL

by Angela McAllister
illustrated by Michaela Bloomfield

DUTTON CHILDREN'S BOOKS   NEW YORK

A long time ago, whales lived not in the ocean but on the land. A whale's life wasn't much fun. All day long, whales lay around pretending to be hills and swallowing unpleasant people to make themselves useful. They didn't go near the sea at all. In fact, whales like Walt and his sister Wisteria hated water. They never took baths, and they stayed in their cave when it rained until every puddle dried up.

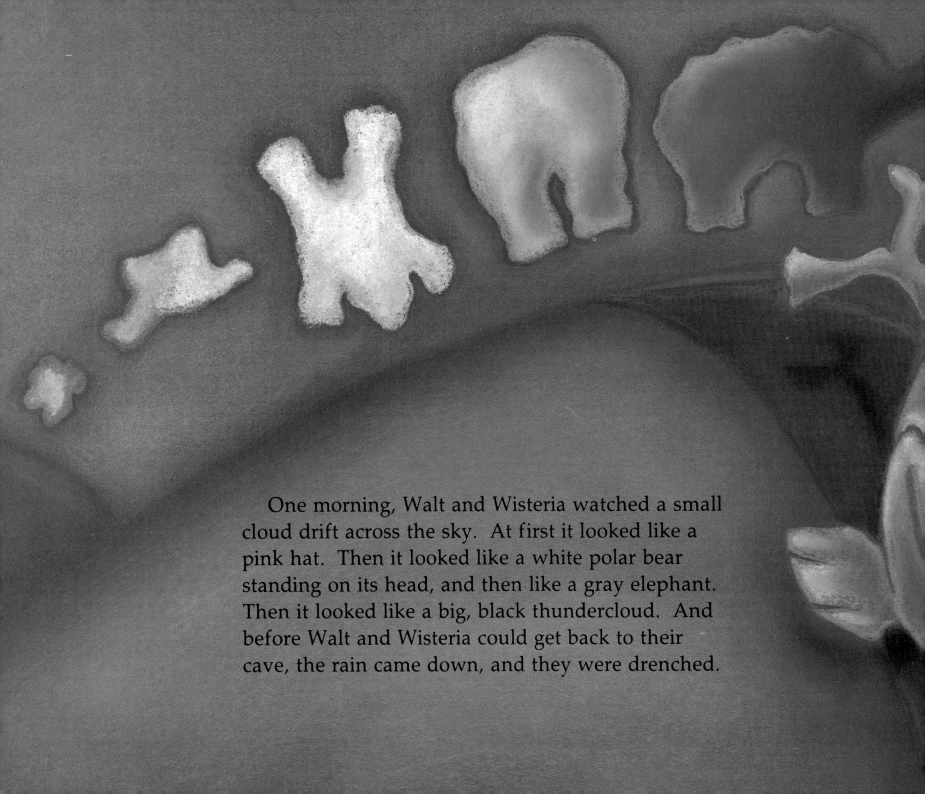

One morning, Walt and Wisteria watched a small cloud drift across the sky. At first it looked like a pink hat. Then it looked like a white polar bear standing on its head, and then like a gray elephant. Then it looked like a big, black thundercloud. And before Walt and Wisteria could get back to their cave, the rain came down, and they were drenched.

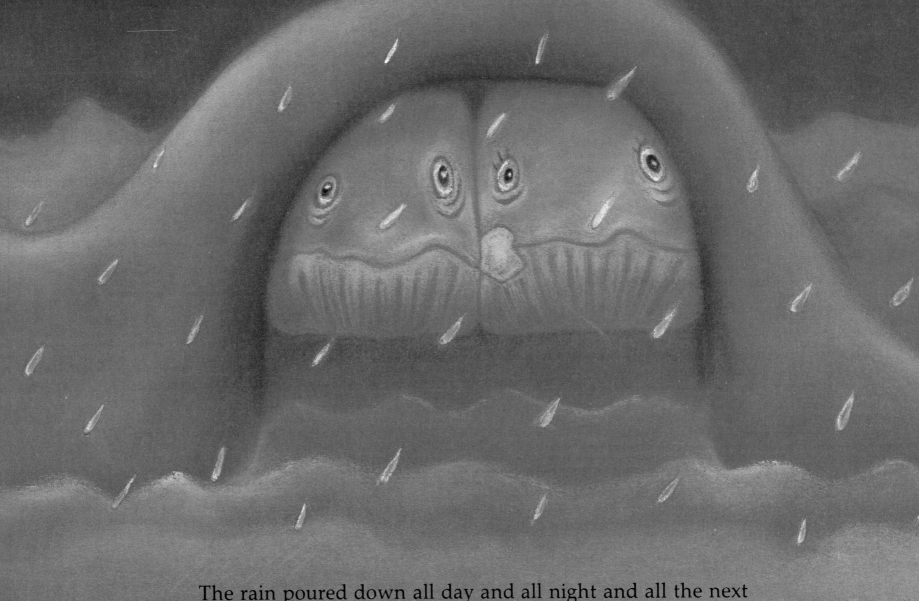

The rain poured down all day and all night and all the next morning. Walt and Wisteria hid in the back of their cave, but the rain trickled in. Before long, the whole cave was flooded. "We've got to find someplace dry," said Wisteria.

"But if we go out, we'll get wet again," cried Walt.

"Well, if we stay here, we'll drown," said Wisteria, trying to be brave. "Follow me."

And so, taking their umbrellas, the whales left their cave to look for a dry place.

Outside, there was water everywhere.
People were splashing around with pots
and pans on their heads.

Nobody wanted to stop and help the whales find an enormous dry place.

Then along came Mr. Noah, rowing a small boat crammed with animals. He was very wet and grumpy. "I was warned about this," he said, shaking his head.

"Can you help us find a dry place?" asked Wisteria.

"Well, I've just built an ark on top of the highest hill," said Noah, wringing the water out of his beard. "And I'm trying to collect the animals, two by two, but everyone's in such a tizzy. Why has everyone gone bananas over a few drops of water?"

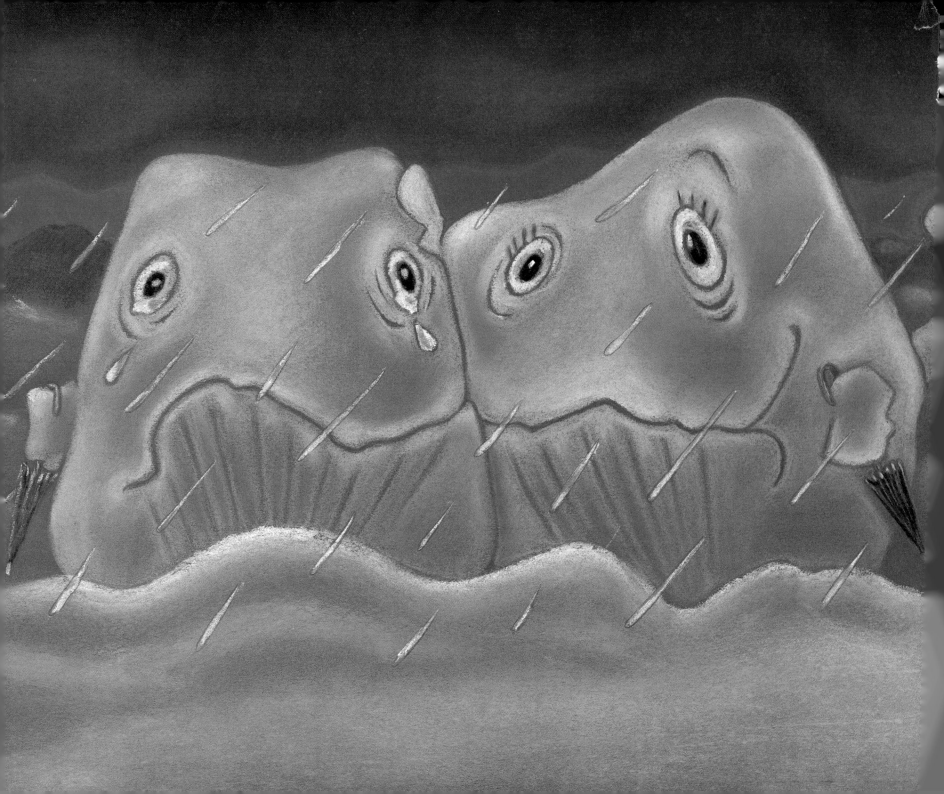

"Is there room for us in your ark?" asked Walt hopefully.

"Follow me up to the top of the hill," said Mr. Noah, feeling sorry for the poor wet whales. "I'll see what I can do. But I'm not making any promises." And off he rowed.

The rain pelted down harder, and the sky grew as black as night.

"Cheer up," said Wisteria. "Soon we'll be nice and dry inside Mr. Noah's big boat."

Walt and Wisteria made their way toward the highest hill. At the top was the most gigantic boat they had ever seen. It was bursting with animals, and even more stood outside, hoping to get in. But Mr. Noah was shaking his head and hammering the door closed.

"I'm sorry, but the ark is full," he said. "Even fuller than full. I just can't help."

As he spoke, lightning shot through the sky, and
the rain poured down heavier than ever.

"Mr. Noah, help us!" cried Wisteria, but the rising
water lifted the boat off the hill, and it floated out of
sight.

Walt and Wisteria clung to each other as the water
rose up to their chins. "Don't let go of me, Wisteria,"
said Walt. But suddenly, he lost his balance and slipped.
And with a huge splash, under the water he went.

All alone and afraid, Wisteria started to wail.

Suddenly, Walt popped out of a huge crashing wave, with a big grin on his face.

"The water is great!" he yelled. "Come on in!"

"*Under* the *water*?" said Wisteria in horror. "I couldn't . . . whoops!" And she slid off the rock and into the water too.

Beneath the surface it was calm and quiet. Wisteria dived and glided, and before she knew it, she was swimming.

"Look at me!" laughed Walt as he turned somersaults.

"Being a whale in the water is much more fun than being a whale on land," said Walt.

Wisteria agreed. "But I wonder what happened to Mr. Noah and his ark," she said.

They swam to the surface. The rain had stopped, and on the horizon they saw Mr. Noah's boat bobbing gently on the sea.

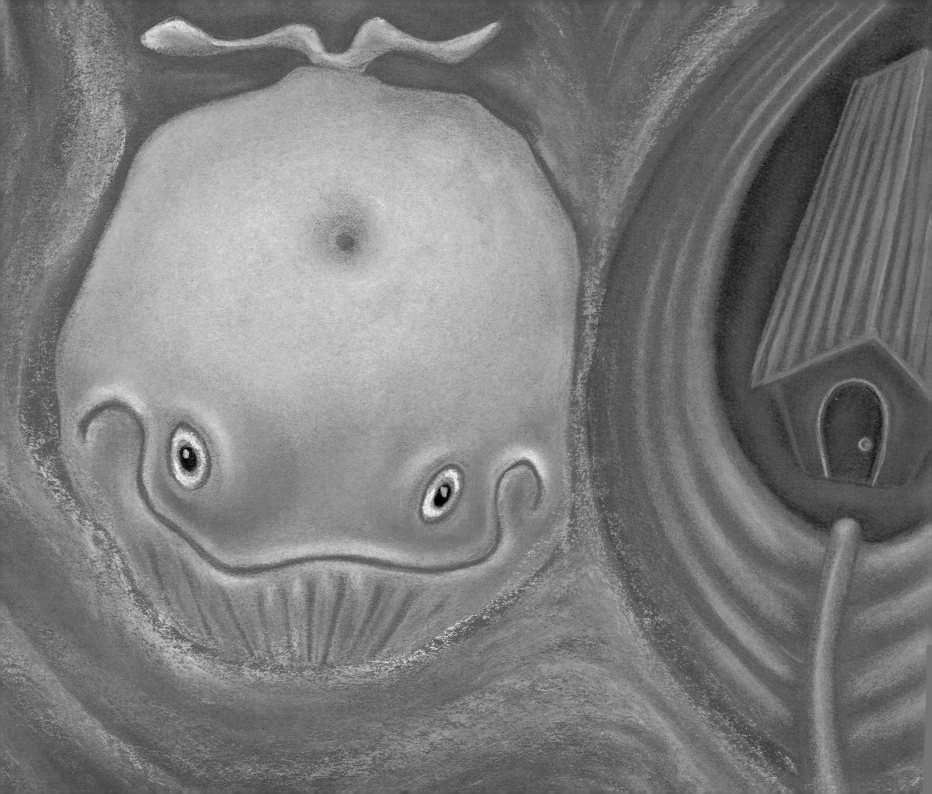

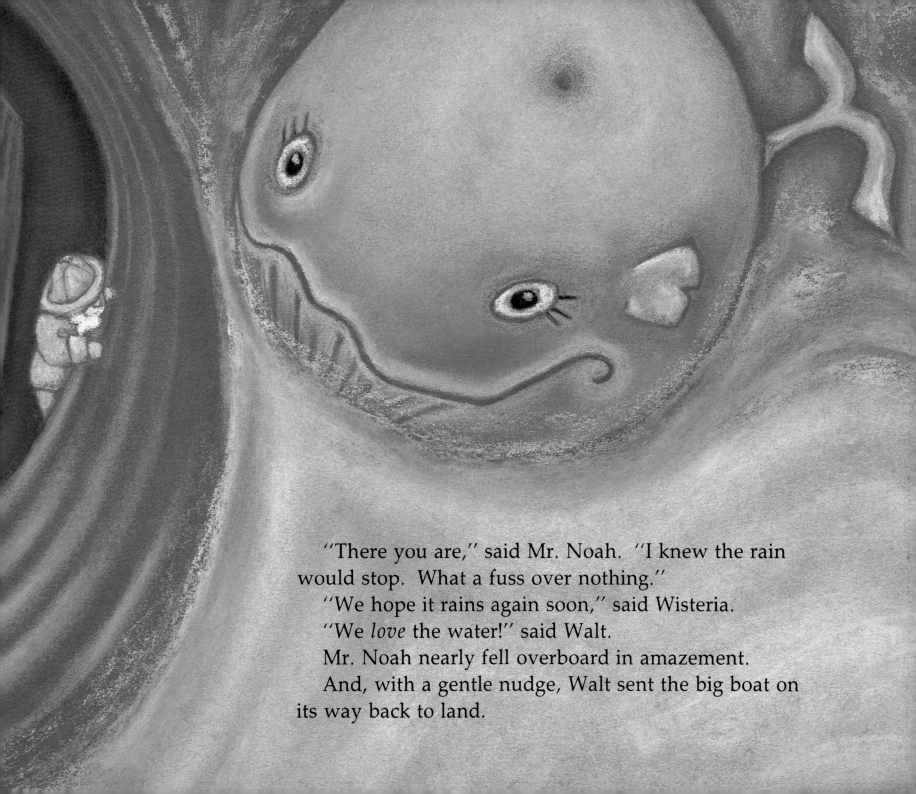

"There you are," said Mr. Noah. "I knew the rain would stop. What a fuss over nothing."

"We hope it rains again soon," said Wisteria.

"We *love* the water!" said Walt.

Mr. Noah nearly fell overboard in amazement.

And, with a gentle nudge, Walt sent the big boat on its way back to land.

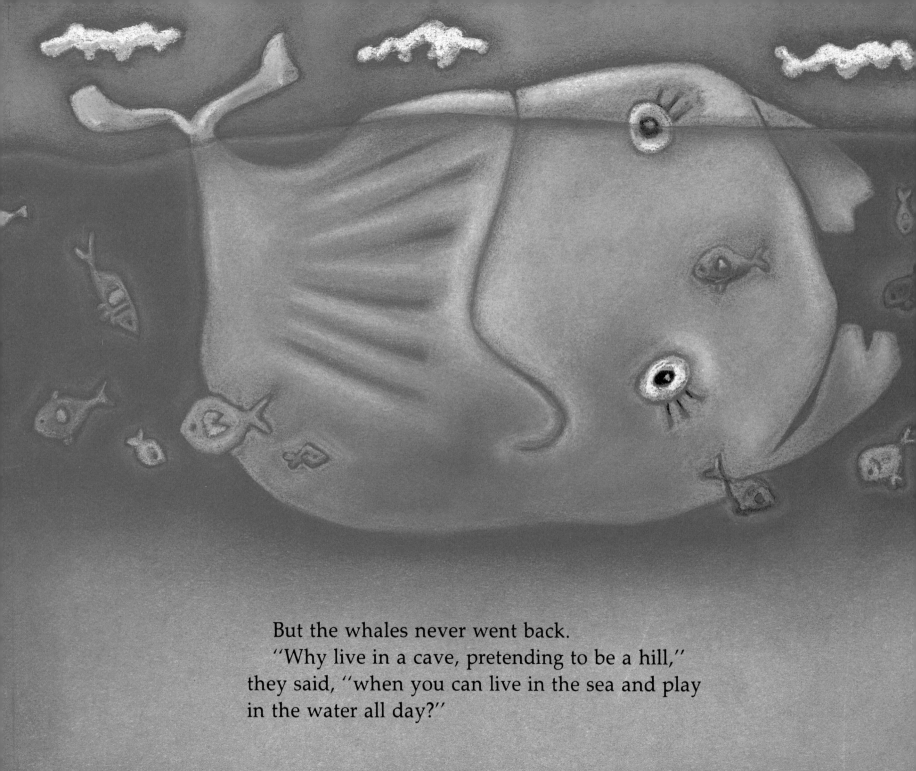

But the whales never went back.
"Why live in a cave, pretending to be a hill,"
they said, "when you can live in the sea and play
in the water all day?"

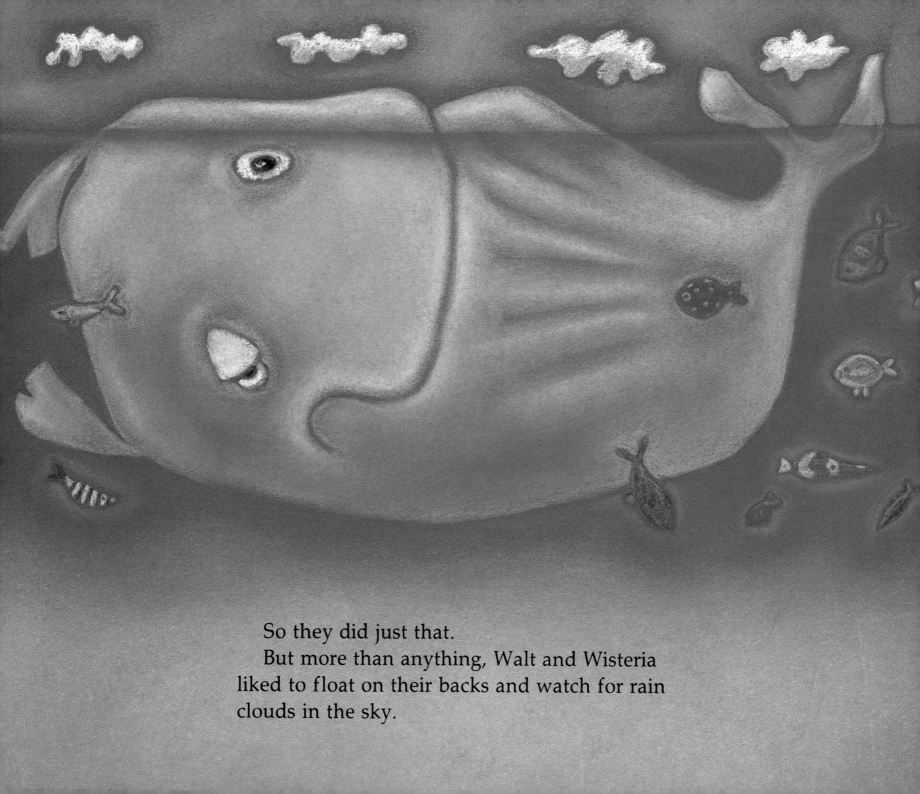

So they did just that.
But more than anything, Walt and Wisteria
liked to float on their backs and watch for rain
clouds in the sky.